For Camille, Joseph, and Lewis.

CALLAWAY

64 Bedford Street
New York, New York 10014

Printed in China by Palace Press International
First Edition
10 9 8 7 6 5 4 3 2 1
Library of Congress Cataloging-in-Publication Data available.

ISBN 0-935112-46-4

Visit Callaway at www.callaway.com

Antoinette White, Senior Editor
Wynn Dan, Art Director
with additional design by Toshiya Masuda and Alston Neal

jean-philippe delhomme

visit
to
another
planet

callaway
new york•2000

We usually go to Connecticut.

But this year, we are taking our family vacation on another planet.

It's a 28-hour spaceflight—nonstop.

On board, Dad reads his travel guide, *A Different Planet,* for the second time. He doesn't like to go to a new place without knowing everything about it. Me? I'm bored. I've already seen all the Mr. Bean films they're showing. To pass the time, I play Space Invaders on my Game Boy.

We're nearly there, at last. The pilot appears on the video screen: "Hello, this is your captain speaking. We are approaching our destination. May I remind you that the artificial gravity light is now off, so please fasten your seatbelts."

Unfortunately, we have to fly in a circle for more than an hour because of heavy air traffic above the airport.

"Is this your first visit to our planet?" a flight attendant asks me. "How exciting! You'll see that everything is very different here."

The airport looks modern enough. Not at all, um, *alien*. We pick up our luggage and head to customs. We've been warned that passengers in possession of a computer must declare it. They are very cautious about computer viruses here. Sometimes PCs or Macs must stay in quarantine, which is sad.

At the exit, some men offer to drive us into town. According to Dad's travel guide, they are illegal taxi drivers. Which means, if we get into an accident, things could become pretty complicated.

The car rental bus stops to pick us up. On board, an electronic voice greets us in five languages: English, Spanish, Japanese, Russian, and one that I don't recognize.

At the rental office, we have the choice of a huge camping van or a little red car. Dad thinks the van would be difficult to park, and Mom and I prefer the red car anyway.

On the highway, my parents are very nervous. Mom is trying to read the map. It's in the local language, which she doesn't know. Dad, who hates video games, says he doesn't feel comfortable driving with a joystick.

A patrolman on a motorcycle stops us. "Begin to accelerate at once," he says in an amplified voice. "You are holding everybody up."

At the hotel, the bellhop who shows us our rooms explains at length that things are very modern here. Instead of keys, they use magnetic cards. I try to tell him that we've got the same thing on Earth, but he pretends not to hear me, and my parents ask me not to insist.

My room is on the 48th floor. I can see a man practicing his golf swing.

Through the other window is an office building. All the people are working late. I bet they're just surfing the Internet.

I can't wait to go outside and look around. But first we have to get some sleep to adjust to the time change, which is two and a half days. So, though it's Monday night here, on Earth it's still only Saturday morning.

I watch TV. The ads are very funny. I don't understand what they're saying, but I think I get the visual jokes.

In the morning, we get up early and go sightseeing. We pass people rushing to work. I wonder whether we look like tourists. Apparently not, because no one pays much attention to us.

By the train station, I buy some little deep-fried seaweed balls from a street vendor. They look odd and have a funny smell, but they taste like chicken.

Next we visit a department store. It's something one ought to do to understand a foreign culture," says Dad. It's a bit disappointing because the store carries the same brands that we have on Earth. They have great sneakers, but everyone looks enviously at my old Nikes. Mom spends ages working out the exchange rate. Stuff is more expensive here, but she buys lots of things anyway. It takes forever to get authorization from Earth for Mom's credit card.

Dad is complaining that everything looks too much like a well-kept shopping mall when we take a wrong turn and end up in an area that is not in the guidebook. Luckily, the car's computer helps us to make a U-turn and get back on the right road.

We return just in time for tea in the hotel lobby with Mr. Mx-Os. He is a longtime business acquaintance of Dad's, though they are meeting face-to-face for the first time. Mr. Mx-Os gives me a present in a very strange box. Unfortunately, it's another Game Boy. But I thank him anyway.

Today, we are going to the countryside.
Dad wants us to see the "real" planet.
On the road we stop to visit a farm.

The farmer gives us some milk. It's just
like the milk we have on Earth, except
it's green and tastes sort of minty.

Then we go on a short hike. We find chewing gum growing wild on the bushes. You're not supposed to pick more than one piece, though, because the area is a nature preserve.

While we are picnicking, little white wild dogs approach us and beg for a bite of our sandwiches. The dogs are so cute. I would like to keep one, but Dad read in the guidebook that they get very homesick. In fact, a law was passed back in 1973 forbidding them to be taken from this planet.

Today, we are going to the mountains. The car's computer doesn't seem to know much about this area. Dad asks a farmworker for directions, using his phrase book. The man answers in English, and he gives us a CD-ROM of maps and information to load onto our car-drive.

When we get to the mountains, we take a shuttle to the top. On this side of the planet, it's always dark and the snow never melts.

Occasionally, we pass an isolated habitation. The shuttle driver explains that people settle here so they can work without distraction. Most are writers or scientists.

The shuttle drops us off at the top. "What a beautiful view!" says Mom. Then we ski down the slope.

I meet a boy who is snowboarding. He has a microtranslator, so we can talk. Our conversation is a little slow, but eventually we understand that we like the same TV show and agree on environmental issues. He writes his name as "%@#‹," which is pronounced "Jack." We exchange email addresses to keep in touch.

On our way back to town, we discover that this planet has huge traffic jams, too. We scan the radio stations, but the music seems to be all the same. Mom thinks it sounds like Swedish rock. "It's got a good beat," says Dad.

We have to stop to recharge the car. While Dad watches the other drivers to figure out how to refuel, Mom and I visit the shop. They sell barbecue units, blankets, and fishing gear, though I haven't seen a single river. I can't resist buying a lot of chocolate bars called Earth.

At a fast-food restaurant, we order hot dogs. They're green but taste pretty normal, especially if you add a lot of ketchup.

Dad says you're only a tourist if you don't get to know the locals. So, we chat with a truck driver who speaks English: "Ah, Earth—a beautiful place! My wife and I went there on our honeymoon. We saw Paris, the pyramids, Venice, Tanzania, Niagara Falls, and Disneyland. Nice people on Earth, all very different from each other—but not that different from us. You know, although we on this planet probably look alike to you, we are all quite different, too."

It's the last day of our vacation. We get to the airport hours early, so we spend time in the souvenir shop. They have dolls, model cars, and wild chewing gum in pretty packages.

We finally decide on green plastic noses.